Write your name here

This book belongs to:

Copyright © 2022 R. Suazon
All rights reserved.
ISBN: 978-0-9939783-3-3

I think my name is super cute! Don't you think so? My human mom likes sunflowers a lot, and I love biscuits very much! And that's why she named me Sunflower Biscuit!

Sitting beside me is Doodle. She calls me Sun-Sun and I call her Bestie. She loves peanut butter so it should have been her name, but her human sister Aliyanah likes to doodle whenever she's bored.

And that's why they named her Doodle!

Doodle and i are next-door neighbors
&
BEST friends forever
#Bffs!
She and I are going to play today.
But first, guess where we are right now?
Hint
farm

If you guessed sunflower farm, you are correct!
I'm glancing at Doodle. She's walking behind me very slowly. I think she's hungry.
These are the sunflowers that my mom picked today. I'm helping her carry them.
That's a biscuit in my hand.

Doodle and I are going to eat our snacks before we play for a little while. Then we will go to my place and play for many, many, MANY hours!
Blueberry infused water
Peanut butter
Biscuits

BY THE WAY

TODAY iS

SUNDAY

My FAVORITE DAY!

"It's my favorite day too!" said Doodle.

WOULD YOU LIKE TO KNOW WHY SUNDAY IS OUR FAVORITE DAY?

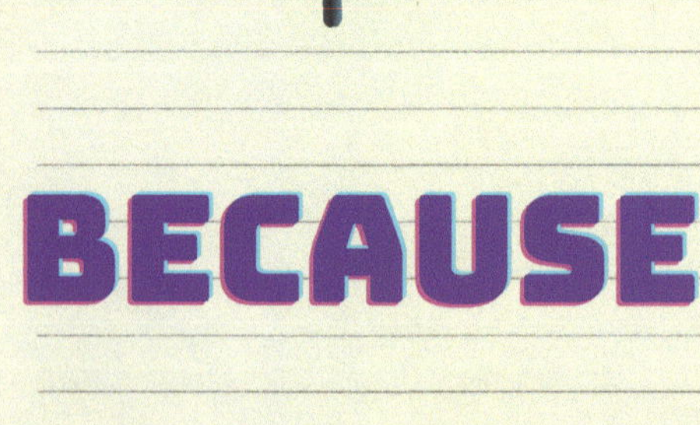
BECAUSE

I will tell you later. Doodle asked me to stop talking because she wants to eat now. She said, "The sooner we eat, the more time we have to play on the farm."

But while you wait, have a look at the Friendship Board on the next page. Aliyanah made it for Doodle's birthday last year.

She's going to make one for me too on my birthday, which is next Sunday! I can't wait! ☺

TTYL

⟨ talk to you later ⟩

Friendship Board
SUNDAY
OUR FAVORITE DAY!
FRIENDSHIP
#Bffs!
BEST friends forever
DOODLE & Sunflower Biscuit

Doodle and I had just finished eating our snacks. The biscuits with peanut butter were delicious!
And the blueberry drink my mommy Rosalia made was very refreshing!

Hi, again!
1
"I'm home now. Doodle and I are in my backyard ready to play some more!"
2
"Sun-Sun, tell them why Sunday is our favorite day!"
3
"Oh yeah, I almost forgot. Thanks for reminding me, Bestie!"
4
"You're welcome!"
5
"Sunday is our favorite day because it's our play-day!"

Sometimes
we play tug-
of-war.

And other times, we play hide-and-seek.

But today, the two of us will play Trick-or-No Treat; it's a game we made up.

I will do 3 tricks.

But one at a time because i can't do them all at the same time. Doodle will try to copy them all. Also one at a time because just like me, she can't do three tricks at the same time.

"What if I can't do them all?" Doodle asked.

"No trick, no treat!" I replied. "You have to do all three tricks, 1 + 1 +1 = 3. That's why the game is called TRICK-OR-NO TREAT!"

"What if I did all 3 tricks?" Doodle also asked.

"Then I will give you a treat that you would like ••• A LOT!" I said to her with a big smile!

DOODLE CHEERED "YAY!"

As if she already knows what I'm going to give her. I think I'll give her the yellow glasses that she really likes, but I'm not going to tell her now. I want her to be surprised!

I said loudly!

Doodle yelled out cheerfully!

TRICK #1

For my first trick, I rolled over.

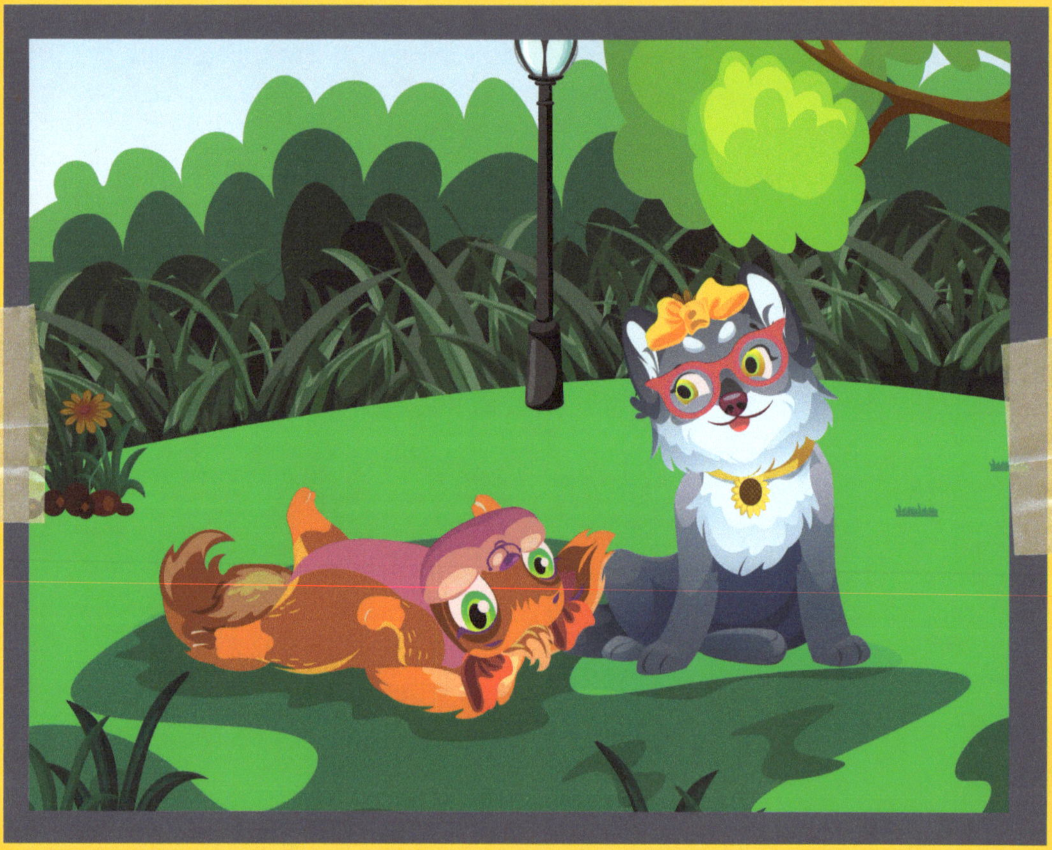

She laid on her back and then she rolled over.

TRICK #2

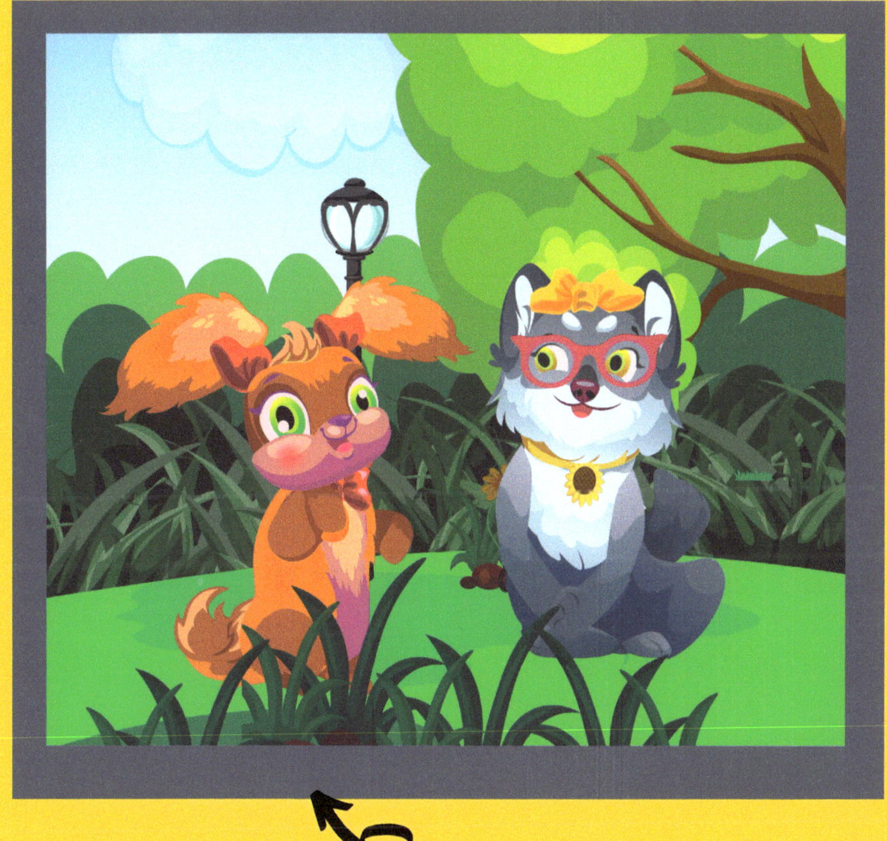

She nodded. For my second trick, I stood on my hind legs and spun slowly. I have never seen her spin so I thought she didn't know how to do it.

But she did it! And she even showed off a little. She stood on her back legs and spun super fast! It's a good thing she didn't lose her balance. She could have broken her bones or something.

TRICK #3

For my third and last trick, I stood on my hind legs again and hopped as high as I could three times in a row.

Doodle hopped too! But she hopped more than three times. She kept on hopping, and yelling "Yippee!" at the same time ... as if she was bouncing on a trampoline.

!

I WANTED TO HAVE FUN too!

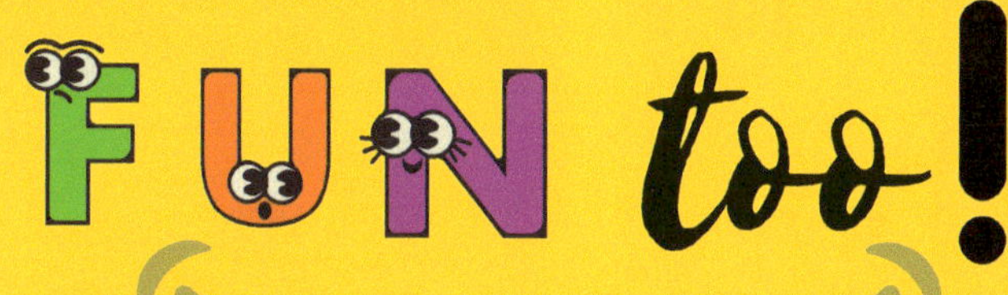

So I stood behind her, and we both jumped around in my backyard like two kangaroos playing in the zoo.

Doodle and I had a lot of fun! But we felt tired afterward, and our paws ached a little.

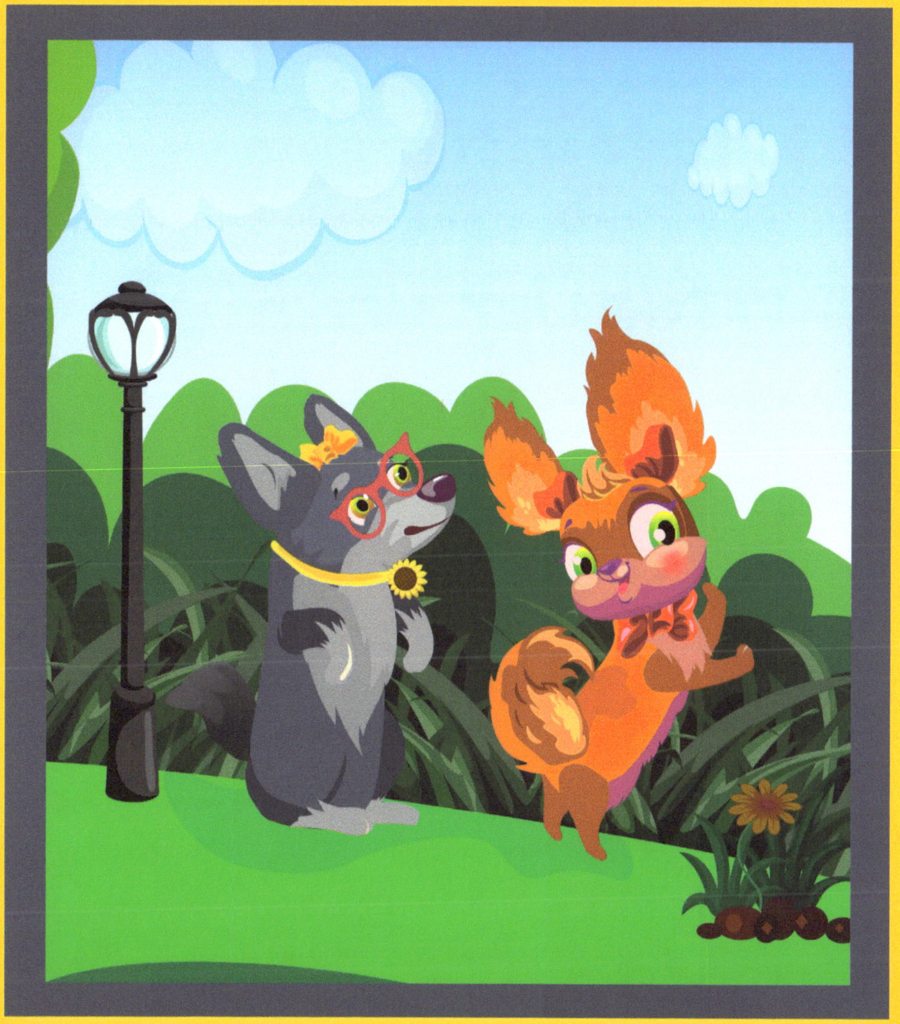

Doodle and i rested.

And then she scratched and scratched her ear.

"Sun-Sun, I had so much fun today!" Doodle said. "Let's call today Fun-Day-Sunday! But my right ear is soooo itchy!"

"Good idea, Bestie! Okay, let's call today Fun-Day-Sunday! Come inside the house after you scratch your ear. I'm going to give you your treat!"

While Doodle scratched her ear, I hurried inside my house to look for the yellow glasses. She tried them on last Sunday and they looked really good on her!

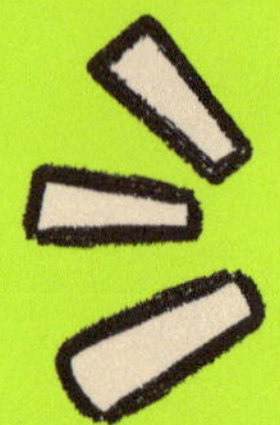

"SURPRISED!" I yelled out! "Here's your treat!"

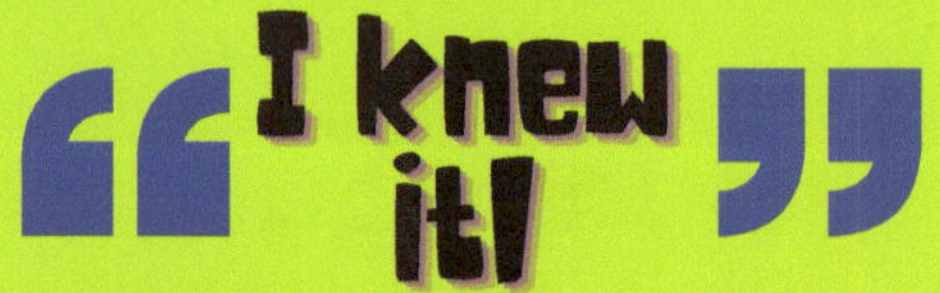

"I knew it!" Doodle said loudly, and MERRILY!

She also said, "Thank you, Sun-Sun! You're the bestest friend in the whole wide world!"

She immediately put on the yellow glasses. Then she hugged me. And then she gave me a big thank-you kiss on my cheek!

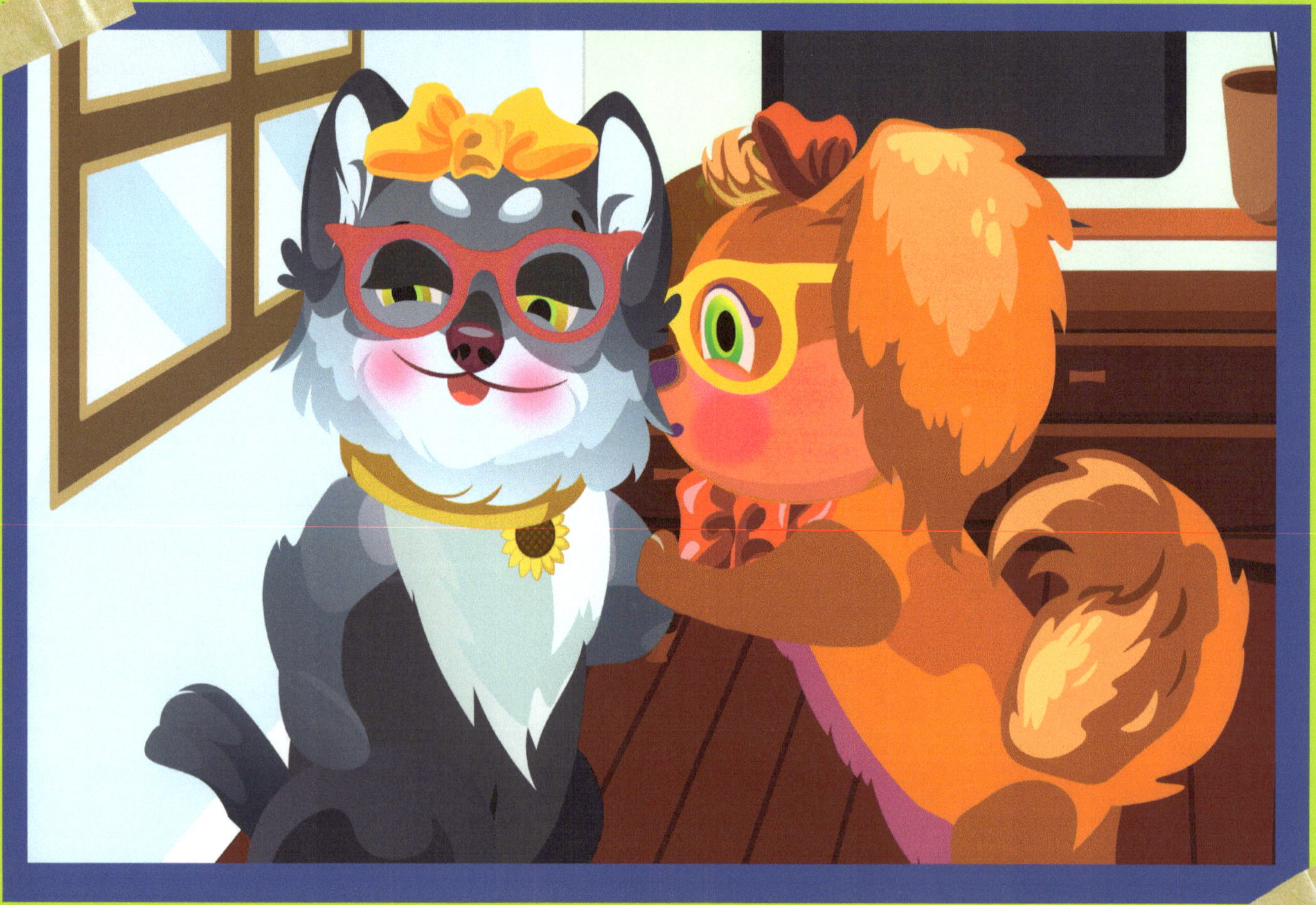

Doodle WAS SO HAPPY!

She swaggered around wearing the yellow glasses like a peacock parading her pretty tail feathers.

I'm glad Doodle did all the tricks I showed her today.   This means she's as smart as me!

As soon as Doodle left with Aliyanah, I took a nap in my bed.

I slept soundly until mommy Rosalia surprised me with a freshly baked biscuit!

She woke me up gently. Then she said while waiving the biscuit near my nose,

"You smell as good as my homemade biscuits and look as pretty as a fresh sunflower in my garden!"

And then she gave me a big  kiss

on my right cheek and said,

And that's why i named you

Sunflower Biscuit ?

The End !
BUT
DON'T CLOSE
THE BOOK
YET
GO
to the
next page

1

2

This is a book about Doodle and her quirky gestures.

I hope you read it too so that she won't feel sad. 

3

your friend,

Sunflower Biscuit

4

The End!
FOR REAL THIS TIME.